With Any Luck, I'll Drive a Truck

DAVID FRIEND
illustrated by MICHAEL REX

Nancy Paulsen Books

For Molly
and all the students
she inspired.
—D.F.

To my mother,
again,
20 years later.
—M.R.

NANCY PAULSEN BOOKS
an imprint of Penguin Random House LLC
375 Hudson Street, New York, NY 10014

Text copyright © 2016 by David Friend. Illustrations copyright © 2016 by Michael Rex.
Penguin supports copyright. Copyright fuels creativity, encourages diverse voices, promotes
free speech, and creates a vibrant culture. Thank you for buying an authorized edition of this book and for complying
with copyright laws by not reproducing, scanning, or distributing any part of it in any form without permission. You
are supporting writers and allowing Penguin to continue
to publish books for every reader.

Nancy Paulsen Books is a registered trademark of Penguin Random House LLC.

Library of Congress Cataloging-in-Publication Data
Friend, David, 1955–
With any luck, I'll drive a truck / David Friend ; illustrated by Michael Rex.
pages cm
Summary: A little boy has a grand time pretending to drive every big vehicle he can imagine.
[1. Stories in rhyme. 2. Trucks—Fiction. 3. Imagination—Fiction.] I. Rex, Michael, illustrator. II. Title. III. Title: With any
luck, I will drive a truck.
PZ8.3.F91165Wi 2016
394.2649—dc22
2015009191

Manufactured in China by RR Donnelley Asia Printing Solutions Ltd.
ISBN 978-0-399-16956-4
3 5 7 9 10 8 6 4

Design by Ryan Thomann. Text set in Kosmik.
The art was created in ink and colored digitally.

At 2,

when I could reach the seat,

I taught myself to make concrete.
I'd crank and mix and stir and scoop,

then set the mold
and spread the goop.

When I got older, 3 or so,
I learned to run a big backhoe.
I'd pull the lever till it hurt

and crunch
that shovel
in the dirt.

I also worked a fireman's truck—
and, sure enough, a cat got stuck!
The kids were sad and I was sadder . . .

until I saved her
with a ladder.

At 4—I know, it sounds insane—
I learned to operate a crane.
The long steel beams I had to lift
made all my muscles creaky stiff.

At 5, it all fell into gear:
That 18-wheeler—I could steer!

That moving van—no problem, man!
That flatbed trailer—YES, I CAN!

It didn't do me any harm
to use a combine on a farm
or, in the dairy, milk a cow . . .

or plow a wheat field with a **plow**.

Earthmover?

Paver?

Forklift, say?
Those too . . .
with time for baling hay!

A huge **jackhammer**?

Bulldozer too?

I manned them all.

At 6, if you would like to know,
I spent the winter plowing snow.

And when the summer came:
a tractor,
dump truck . . .
and a trash compactor.

But now I'm 7, and I've got
a bedroom like a parking lot.
And if I can, when I turn 10,
or maybe *twice* the age as then—

When I grow up . . . you know wassup.
With any luck, I'll drive a truck.